SNOWBOARD DUEL

Bob Temple

illustrated by Sean Tiffany

Librarian Reviewer
Chris Kreie, Media Specialist

Reading Consultant
Mary Evenson, Teacher

H 00 2538286

Schools Library Service

www.raintreepublishers.co.uk
Visit our website to find out
more information about
Raintree books.

To order:
☎ Phone 0845 6044371
🖷 Fax +44 (0) 1865 312263
🖳 Email myorders@capstonepub.co.uk

Customers from outside the UK please telephone +44 1865 312262

Raintree is an imprint of Capstone Global Library Limited, a company
incorporated in England and Wales having its registered office at 7 Pilgrim
Street, London, EC4V 6LB – Registered company number: 6695582

"Raintree" is a registered trademark of Pearson Education Limited,
under licence to Capstone Global Library Limited

Text © Stone Arch Books, 2008
First published in the United Kingdom
by Capstone Global Library in 2010
The moral rights of the proprietor have been asserted.

All rights reserved. No part of this publication may be reproduced in
any form or by any means (including photocopying or storing it in
any medium by electronic means and whether or not transiently or
incidentally to some other use of this publication) without the written
permission of the copyright owner, except in accordance with the
provisions of the Copyright, Designs, and Patents Act 1988 or under
the terms of a licence issued by the Copyright Licensing Agency,
Saffron House, 6–10 Kirby Street, London EC1N 8TS (www.cla.co.uk).
Applications for the copyright owner's written permission should be
addressed to the publisher.

Edited in the UK by Laura Knowles
Art Director: Heather Kindseth
Graphic Designer: Kay Fraser
Originated by Capstone Global Library
Printed and bound in China by Leo Paper Products Ltd

ISBN 978 1 406213 75 1 (hardback)
14 13 12 11 10
10 9 8 7 6 5 4 3 2 1

ISBN 978 1 406213 96 6 (paperback)
14 13 12 11 10
10 9 8 7 6 5 4 3 2 1

British Library Cataloguing in Publication Data
Temple, Bob.
Snowboard duel. -- (Sport stories)
813.6-dc22
A full catalogue record for this book is available from the British Library.

Disclaimer
All the Internet addresses (URLs) given in this book were valid at the
time of going to press. However, due to the dynamic nature of the
Internet, some addresses may have changed, or sites may have changed
or ceased to exist since publication. While the author and publishers
regret any inconvenience this may cause readers, no responsibility for
any such changes can be accepted by either the author or the publishers.

CONTENTS

CHAPTER 1

NEW RULES

The door of the bus had barely closed behind him, and Max was on his way to the chalet.

It was the way Max ended almost every school day, jumping off the bus and heading at full speed to the slopes.

Max's mother was the assistant manager of Snowstream Ski Resort. That meant Max had easy access to the resort's many cool features.

Each day, he would head straight for the chalet. He would open his locker and pull out his snowboard gear. He would rush to put it on, and would get to the slopes as quickly as he could.

On the slopes, he would meet his friends. Almost all of them were kids whose parents worked at the resort. Most of them were about Max's age, and they were all snowboarders.

Some days were spent at the half-pipe, working on a front side 720 or another special trick. Other days were spent grinding the rails down the slopes.

No matter what they were doing, Max and his friends were happy.

Max often snowboarded until dark. Then he would head home for a late dinner and homework before bed.

The next morning, the whole thing would start again.

It was a great life.

Max popped in to his mother's office to say hello before he headed for the chairlift. He bolted toward the office on the top floor of the chalet.

"Hey, Mum," Max said as he came through the door.

"Hi, Max," his mum responded. She seemed a little busy.

"I'm going to the half-pipe today, okay?" Max said.

"Okay," she said, barely looking up from her papers. "Have fun."

His mum had been busy a lot since the resort manager retired three months ago.

They hadn't replaced him yet, and it meant that Max's mum had a lot of extra work to do.

Max grabbed his board on the deck of the chalet and bounced down the steps toward the snow. He stepped into his bindings and latched the right boot in place. Pushing along the snow with his left foot, he glided down towards the chairlift.

His best friend, Hannah, was there waiting for him. "Hey, Max," she said. Hannah seemed a little distracted.

The lifts weren't busy, so Max and Hannah got on a chair quickly. Once they were up in the air, Max started asking questions.

"You okay?" he said. "You seem a little down."

"Well, didn't you hear the news? Didn't your mum tell you?" Hannah asked.

"Tell me what?" Max asked.

"I ran into my dad on my way here," Hannah said. Hannah's father ran the restaurant in the chalet. "I guess the resort hired a new manager," Hannah added.

"Oh, good!" Max said. "My mum's been waiting for that. Maybe now she won't have to work so much."

"I don't know about that," Hannah said. "My dad said the new manager's not a very nice person. She's making a bunch of new rules straight away."

"Like what?" Max said.

"Like, we may not be able to snowboard for free anymore," she said.

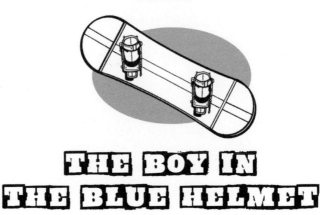

CHAPTER 2

THE BOY IN THE BLUE HELMET

Max sat quietly on the chair for a few moments.

It was a crisp, calm day. The growing chill he was feeling was not from the weather.

"What do you mean?" he finally asked.

Hannah glanced across the slopes. Below them, skiers were swooshing down the mountain through the soft, fluffy snow that had fallen only hours earlier.

"Being able to use the resort for free is a benefit that our parents have, and we have, because of their jobs," Hannah said.

"I know that, but why would they take it away?" Max said.

"I don't know," Hannah said. "All I know is what my dad told me. The new manager said she wanted to make some changes to the benefits that the families of the employees get."

Silence again fell over the chairlift. Hannah and Max could see the end of the chairlift now.

They both wondered if they were soon going to see the end of their time on the slopes, too.

Then Max said what both of them were thinking.

"But if we lose the free snowboarding," he said, "what are we going to do all winter? What else are we going to do up here on this mountain?"

Hannah just shook her head.

Both of them slipped off the chairlift and pushed over to the top of the nearby half-pipe.

At the edge of the pipe, they paused and looked at each other.

They both shook their heads and started down the run.

As soon as they swooped down one side of the half-pipe, their minds were free again.

Max led the way as they played a game they called Chase.

They had played many times before.

One of them would go out in front and do a trick on each side of the pipe.

The other would follow behind, watching and trying to match everything the leader did.

Chase was a game they had been playing for two winters, ever since both of their parents had been hired at Snowstream.

Hannah and Max loved the game so much that they didn't even have to talk about playing it anymore.

If they were at the half-pipe, they were playing Chase.

On the first run, Max didn't try anything too hard, but their first time down was usually pretty relaxed.

Hannah didn't have much trouble matching Max, trick for trick. She rarely did anyway.

Hannah was as good a snowboarder as Max was.

There were a few tricks he could do better and a few she could do better.

When they got to the bottom of the run, they came together and gave each other a high five.

"Great run," Hannah said. "Next time, I lead."

They looked up the half-pipe and talked about the tricks they had tried and how they had done.

Suddenly, however, there was a new figure at the top of the half-pipe.

It was hard to see who it was from the bottom of the run, but the person didn't look familiar to Hannah and Max.

He wore a full, dark-blue snowboarding suit, with a helmet to match.

Hannah and Max watched the new boy's run.

He zoomed back and forth on the half-pipe at top speed.

At each turn, he performed a different trick, making each one look more effortless than the one before it.

It was a beautiful run.

At the bottom of the run, the boy zoomed up to Hannah and Max.

He leaned back on his board to come to a stop.

Snow flew all over their boots in the process.

"Nice run!" Hannah said politely.

"Hmph," the boy snorted back. "That's not much of a half-pipe."

CHAPTER 3

MAKING CHANGES

Max and Hannah glanced at each other, shocked.

They weren't sure they heard the boy right, and they weren't sure what to say to him.

"I'm sorry, is there something wrong?" Max said, still trying to be polite.

"Yeah, I'd say so," the boy said. "Your half-pipe is weak."

Hannah looked the boy up and down.

He was tall, and looked a little older than them.

His snowboarding suit was perfectly matched and looked nearly brand new and expensive.

The trousers and the jacket both had the same logo: Blair Mountain Ski Resort.

This wasn't normal clothing that you could buy at the resort, either. It looked like some kind of team outfit.

Both Hannah and Max recognized it.

Blair Mountain was one of the best and most expensive resorts in the Rocky Mountains.

Neither Hannah nor Max had ever been there.

But they had both talked about how cool it would be to go and snowboard there someday.

The ski runs were supposed to be twice as long as the ones at Snowstream.

The boy's board was top of the range, too. Hannah and Max didn't have the gear that this new boy had.

They both wore red Snowstream jackets, but they were the normal kind you could find at a store. Nothing special.

Their snowboard pants didn't match their coats, and they had been bought from a discount store on the Internet.

Their boards were average brands, too.

None of that had ever mattered to Max and Hannah until this boy turned up.

Both of them felt a little jealous of the boy, but they weren't ready to accept the insult to their home.

"Weak?" Hannah said. "It may not be Blair Mountain, but we like it here."

"Well, we need to make some changes," the boy said.

Now Max was getting angry. "We? We need to make some changes?"

"That's what I said," the boy said. "We need to make some changes around here."

The boy reached down and unstrapped his snowboard from his back leg.

He began to push down toward the chairlift again.

Max and Hannah looked at each other in amazement.

Neither one of them was sure what to do next.

Max headed after the boy. "Excuse me," he yelled.

The boy kept walking to the chairlift.

"Excuse me!" Max shouted.

This time, the boy stopped.

"Just who exactly do you think you are, hotshot?" Max asked. He could feel that his face was red with anger.

The boy spun back with a sly smile on his face.

"I'm Zach," he said. "My mum is the new manager here. And like I said, we need to make a few changes."

CHAPTER 4

FREE NO MORE

Suddenly, Max and Hannah didn't feel much like boarding.

They glided back to the chalet and unstrapped their snowboards. Then they stomped up the back steps to the chalet's deck, took off their boots, and went inside.

They spent the rest of the afternoon sitting by the fire in the chalet, talking about this new boy and what the new rules might mean.

"We need some kind of a plan," Max said.

"How can we make a plan if we don't know what's going to happen yet?" Hannah said. "We should be patient and see what he's up to, then make our plan." Max agreed.

Gradually, all of their other friends started to show up in the chalet. Tom, Aaron, and Will had each already had some kind of run-in with Zach. They were all looking for information about what might be happening. And they wanted to share their stories with friends.

"He asked me if I could grind the rails on the snowboard runs," Tom said. "I said yes and then showed him. When I got to the bottom of the hill, he was laughing at me."

The others had similar stories.

No one was sure what to make of it. But they all figured they'd find out soon enough.

* * *

That night at home, Max tried to talk to his mum about Zach.

She was sympathetic, but said there wasn't much that could be done just now.

"I'm sure he's just trying to look cool in his new home," she said. "He'll tone it down once he gets to know all of you."

Max wasn't so sure.

"He keeps talking about changes," Max said. "And Hannah told me that her dad said we might lose our right to free snowboarding. Is that true?"

"I don't know yet, Max," his mom said. She sighed. "But I'm sure that some things will change. Things always change when there is a new manager. It's nothing to worry about."

But Max was still worried.

* * *

After school the next day, he and Hannah met at the resort again.

They walked into the locker room and got ready to snowboard.

On their way out to the slopes, however, they saw Zach inside the chalet.

He was putting up a sign on the bulletin board. In bold letters, it read:

TEEN SNOWBOARD CROSS

TEAM SIGN-UP

There was an empty space below it for people to put their names.

Hannah and Max were confused, because Snowstream didn't have a snowboard cross course on it.

But they were both excited, too. They had always wanted to try snowboard cross. The idea of racing against other people down a twisting, turning snowboard run sounded pretty cool.

Hannah saw it as a chance to be nice to Zach. "Hey, Zach. So you're starting a snowboard cross team? Here at Snowstream?" she asked him.

"Yeah," he said. He didn't seem interested in her questions. "I was captain of the team at Blair Mountain. We were winners. Even though I'm stuck at this resort now, I still want to win."

Hannah and Max tried to ignore the nasty part of Zach's comments.

"Sounds like fun," Max said.

"It's awesome," Zach said. "My mum said we're going to take one of the ski runs and turn it into a snowboard cross course. We'll be able to start practicing in a few weeks. And I'm the captain."

CHAPTER 5

GETTING AIR

Hannah and Max started to feel a little differently about Zach after they found out about the snowboard cross team.

They weren't sure they liked the idea of Zach being the captain. But they thought being on the team would be fun.

They were the first two people to put their names on the sign-up sheet.

Tom, Aaron, and Will all signed up, too.

For the next couple of weeks, the mood at Snowstream was better.

Every day after school, and all day on weekends, the kids snowboarded on the slopes and the half-pipe.

Their worries about changes to the rules about free skiing were gone.

After all, if Snowstream was starting a teen snowboard cross team, they would have to allow those kids to use the resort.

Max and Hannah didn't see much of Zach.

When they did, he was over on the run that was being turned into a snowboard cross course.

The area had been closed to the public. It looked like Zach was helping the workers test the course.

Finally, one day they arrived at the slopes to find the snowboard cross course open. They couldn't wait to give it a try.

They rushed to get their snowboard suits and boots on, and quickly headed towards the chairlifts.

"Have you heard anything about it?" Hannah asked as they rode up the side of the mountain.

"Not much," Max said. "My mum said it was going to be really hard. That's all I know."

"Sounds fun to me!" Hannah said.

Max couldn't remember a time when he saw her so excited.

When they got to the drop-off point for the chairlift, Hannah cruised over towards the top of the course.

Max struggled to keep up. "Wait up!" he yelled.

"Not a chance," Hannah shot back. "I'm not letting you take the course first!"

"Well," Max responded, "it is a race course. Maybe you and I should have a little race!"

Hannah wasn't going to miss a chance to race against her best friend.

Both of them saw the beginnings of a great new game.

It could be every bit as fun as Chase was at the half-pipe.

Hannah waited for Max at the top of the run.

There was no official way to start them, so they just counted to three.

"One, two, three!" they yelled, and off they went.

The early part of the course was full of sharp, high-banked turns that they both handled easily.

Hannah took a better path, and moved a little bit ahead of Max.

Coming around the third turn, they ran into a series of moguls.

Max kept his balance, bent his knees, and bounced over the small mounds quickly.

Hannah wasn't prepared for them and stumbled over the first few. She didn't fall, but losing her balance allowed Max to pull ahead.

Over the next few straightaways and turns, Max kept his small advantage.

He cruised over some angled bumps, or spines, making small jumps off each one.

Finally, he and Hannah navigated the last turn and headed down the steep, straight slope towards the finish line.

Only one jump remained. Max took it hard, getting as much air as he could.

He loved to feel the rush of sailing high into the sky. Hannah did, too, but she knew that getting too much air would only slow her down.

She stayed low, sailing off the jump only a few feet but further down the mountain.

When they both landed, they were in nearly the same place.

When they crossed the finish line, it was too close to call.

They both skidded to a stop. "That was brilliant!" Hannah yelled.

"Glad you liked it," came a voice. It was Zach. He was looking directly at Hannah. "Because it's going to be your last run."

CHAPTER 6

THE NUMBER ONE RULE

Hannah and Max couldn't believe what they were hearing.

Just minutes before, they had been so excited as they zoomed down the mountain.

Now, they were confused and upset.

"What?" Max said, struggling to figure out what to say. "What do you mean? Why is it our last run?"

"Oh, not for you," Zach said. Then he pointed at Hannah. "For her."

Zach started to glide away on his board.

"Hold on a minute," Max called after him. "What are you talking about?"

Zach stopped in his tracks. He spun back towards them. His face was angry, but he had a bit of a smirk, too.

"Look," he said. "I'll make this simple for you. Our snowboard cross team has one simple rule: No girls."

Hannah and Max looked at each other, completely confused.

Hannah had heard from her parents about times when girls weren't allowed to do a lot of the things that boys were allowed to do.

But those times were long gone.

Hannah had never been told she couldn't do something just because she was a girl.

She had no idea what to say.

Max was just plain angry.

"You can't do that, Zach, even if your mum is the manager!" he yelled. "That's discrimination!"

Zach laughed out loud. "I can do whatever I want," he said. "If it wasn't for me, there would be no team. And I'm not going to be caught snowboarding on the same team with any girls."

Max was astonished. "Are you kidding?" he said. "You're kidding, right? Even you can't be this mean."

"It's not about being mean," Zach said.

"I want to win. Full stop. That's all I care about," Zach added. "And I can't win if I have a girl on my team."

Max was trying to stay calm. He thought he might have a way to reason with Zach.

"Hey, listen, you're making a mistake," he said. "Hannah's as good a skier and snowboarder as any of us out here. It shouldn't matter if she's a girl, as long as she's good enough. And she's more than good enough."

Zach's response was quick. "I don't care," he said.

Now Max was back to being angry. "Well, I do care," he said. "I care a lot. And so do the other kids here."

Max was moving towards Zach as he spoke. By the time he was done, he was in Zach's face. "If Hannah can't be on the team, then none of us will be, either," Max said. "You won't have a team at all!"

Max backed up a bit. He felt like he had made his point.

Zach let out a sigh. "Well, that would be a shame," he said. "Because my mum made a new rule at the resort: The only kids who get free snowboarding are the kids on the snowboard cross team."

CHAPTER 7

STANDING STRONG

Max and Hannah were speechless.

Zach gave another sly smile, turned, and headed for the chairlift. "Time for another run," he said. "I need to get used to this new course."

As Zach sailed away, Max and Hannah stood there, staring at each other.

Once again, they found themselves feeling like they didn't want to snowboard.

They glided back towards the chalet, unstrapped their snowboards, and walked inside.

Neither of them said a word. They walked to the snack counter and ordered hot chocolate. Then they found a warm seat in the chalet.

Hannah was a bundle of emotions.

She was angry at Zach for his new rules.

She was worried that her friendship with Max was going to cost him his chance to snowboard.

And she was worried that she, too, would have to finish snowboarding forever.

Finally, she found the words she wanted to say. "Max, you've got to be on the team," she said.

"Not if you can't be on it," Max responded.

"But if you don't, you won't be able to snowboard at all," Hannah said.

"I know," Max said. "But what Zach's doing isn't right. We have to figure out a way to fight this."

"How can we?" Hannah said. "We can't ask our parents to help, because his mum is the new manager."

Both of them sighed.

Just then, the other kids arrived in the chalet. They had just run into Zach on the snowboard cross course, too.

"We heard about the snowboard cross team," Aaron said. "Sorry to hear you can't be on the team. We'll really miss snowboarding with you."

"What do you mean?" Max said, rising to his feet. "Are you saying you are going to be on the team?"

"We have to," Will said. "Otherwise, we can't snowboard at all."

Hannah shrank into her seat. She couldn't even look at the boys.

"So you would turn on your friend, just to keep snowboarding?" Max said. The anger rose in his voice.

"It's not our fault," Aaron said. "We didn't make the stupid rule."

Suddenly, Zach appeared in the chalet. "Are you guys coming?" he called. "Our first team practice starts in fifteen minutes."

The three boys looked back at Hannah and Max. "Come on, Max," Will said.

"I'm not going anywhere," said Max.

The three boys left with Zach. None of them looked back to see Hannah's face.

Max, his anger still bubbling on the surface, looked at Hannah. "I can't believe those guys," he said.

"Aw, forget about them," Hannah said. "You can't blame them for wanting to keep snowboarding."

"I know, but I'm not going to sit here and just take this," he said. "We have to work out a way to challenge this."

Suddenly, Hannah's face brightened. "That's it!" she shouted. "I'll challenge him! There's no way he'd back down from a challenge."

CHAPTER 8

SHOWDOWN

Hannah and Max bolted from the chalet as fast as they could.

They grabbed their boards and headed back outside and towards the snowboard cross course.

"Are you sure you want to do this?" Max asked. "He's pretty good, and he's got way more snowboard cross experience than you do."

"I don't care," Hannah said.

They rushed to the chairlift and hopped on a chair.

The ride seemed to take forever.

As they rode up the lift, Hannah practiced the words she would say to Zach when she saw him.

When they hopped off the chairlift and headed to the course, they saw Zach right away.

He was at the top of the course, talking to the three other boys.

He was giving them advice on tackling the course.

Hannah cruised over to him and used only two words: "Prove it."

"Prove what?" Zach said. "I've got nothing to prove."

"Prove that I don't belong on the team," Hannah shot back. "Race me."

"Why would I do that?" Zach said.

"All I'm asking for is a chance," she said. "You win, and I won't bother you again. I win, and I'm on the team."

With that, the other boys chimed in.

"Come on, Zach," Tom said. "Give her a chance. It's only fair."

Zach took a deep breath. "Fine," he said. "Whatever. If I have to blow you away to make you stop complaining, I'll do it."

Hannah was a little surprised.

She hadn't been sure she'd be able to convince Zach to race her.

After all, he had nothing to gain by doing it.

As they moved over to the start of the course, Zach turned to his three new teammates. "I'll get this over with once and for all," he muttered.

At the starting line, Zach stared directly at Hannah.

Hannah looked a little nervous. But Max gave her some final words of encouragement.

"Come on, Hannah," he said. "You can do this."

Will agreed to be the starter, and he counted to three.

The snowboarders took off quickly, but Zach got the faster jump.

He immediately cut in front of Hannah, nearly knocking her board off track in the process.

Zach held the early lead through the first set of hairpin turns.

Every time Hannah tried to move past him, Zach quickly changed his course to cut her off.

They zoomed around the third turn and into the moguls.

Max could tell that Hannah had learned a lesson from her earlier run.

This time, she stayed low and let her knees absorb the bumps.

She zoomed to the outside of the track to try to pass Zach.

Zach again moved to cut her off, but this time he was too late.

Hannah was alongside him.

Still, Zach pushed outward.

Hannah neared the edge of the course and lost her balance.

Zach continued to push out until Hannah had no choice but to leave the course.

She tumbled off to the side as Zach continued down the hill, laughing.

Zach yelled, "Whoo!" as he cruised away.

Hannah didn't give up, even though she knew it was hopeless. She got back on her feet and back on the course.

By then Zach was two full turns ahead of her. Now, he was doing tricks on the run, showing off.

Hannah lost sight of him as she made the final turn.

He probably already finished the course, she thought.

But when she approached the final jump, she saw him.

He was sprawled across the jump.

He was reaching down towards one of his legs.

He seemed to be in a lot of pain.

Hannah slid up to him and turned her board to the side, coming to a stop alongside Zach.

"Are you all right?" she said.

"My ankle . . . my ankle," Zach said.

"Here, let me help you," Hannah said, bending down to grab Zach's hand.

Zach looked shocked. "Don't you want to win the race?" he asked.

"It's okay," Hannah said. "Let's get down the hill and over to the first aid office. Come on."

Zach was amazed.

Hannah just smiled.

She helped Zach to his feet.

Then she let him lean on her as they gently glided down the rest of the course.

Hannah turned to Zach after they crossed the finish line together.

"So, did I win?" she said, smiling.

Zach didn't say anything.

Hannah could tell he was thinking, hard.

Soon, Max and the other boys joined them at the bottom of the hill.

None of them had seen what happened.

"Who won?" Max asked urgently.

Hannah opened her mouth to speak, but Zach interrupted.

"She did," he said.

Only Zach and Hannah knew what really happened. Zach looked at Hannah, and then said, "She's on the team."

ABOUT THE AUTHOR

Bob Temple has written more than thirty books for children. Over the years, he has coached more than twenty kids' football, basketball, and baseball teams. He also loves visiting classrooms to talk about his writing.

ABOUT THE ILLUSTRATOR

When Sean Tiffany was growing up, he lived on a small island. Every day, he had to take a boat to get to school. When Sean isn't working on his art, he works on a multimedia project called "OilCan Drive", which combines music and art. He has a pet cactus named Jim.

GLOSSARY

chairlift line of chairs hanging above the ground that carries skiers and snowboarders to the tops of the hills

chalet lodge at a skiing resort, for visitors to go when they are not skiing

course track or route on which a race of some kind is run

frontside snowboard trick that starts with the rider facing forwards

grind to glide across a rail on a snowboard

half-pipe U-shaped ramp used by snowboarders to provide a take-off for jumps and tricks

mogul mound of hard snow

rail bar that is raised above the ground that snowboarders use to glide across

straightaway straight course or track

MORE ABOUT...

Snowboard Cross is a relatively new sport. Snowboarding was a popular sport that grew into an Olympic-level competitive sport in the 1990s. But Snowboard Cross became an Olympic sport for the first time in the 2006 Olympics in Torino, Italy.

Unlike other snowboarding competitions, snowboard cross isn't judged.

Competitors race down a course, trying to beat each other to the finish line. Unlike other skiing events, competitors race against each other at the same time. Some people say it's a little like BMX bike racing, only on snow.

In the first rounds of the Olympics, snowboard cross racers make timed runs down the course. The racers with the fastest times make the final rounds, thirty-two racers in all.

...SNOWBOARD CROSS

The excitement grows in the final rounds, when riders race in groups of four. The top two racers in each heat make it to the next round, until only four riders remain. The final four ride in one last race, with the winner taking the gold medal.

Snowboard Cross was an instant hit in its first Olympics. Fans liked watching the riders compete on the course at the same time. The bumping and positioning during the head-to-head racing made it very exciting.

In the 2006 Olympics, American Seth Wescott won the gold medal for men. Radoslav Zidek of Slovakia won the silver medal, and Paul-Henri Delerue of France took bronze. In the women's final, Tanja Frieden of Switzerland won the gold medal, Lindsey Jacobellis of the U.S. won the silver medal, and Dominique Maltais of Canada earned the bronze.

DISCUSSION QUESTIONS

1. How do you think Zach could have handled the situation at the new resort better?

2. Hannah challenged Zach to a race to get on the team. How else could she have convinced him?

3. Will, Aaron, and Tom chose being on the team over their friendship with Hannah. What would you have done? Did they have any other choices?

4. Why do you think Zach didn't want any girls on the team?

WRITING PROMPTS

1. Because of their parents' jobs, Max and Hannah spent their time in a different way from most kids their age. Has your parent or guardian's job ever affected you? Write about it.

2. Max stood up for Hannah. Write about a time when you stood up for someone, or when someone stood up for you.

3. Zach fell at the end because he was showing off. Write about a time when you made a bad decision and paid a price for it.

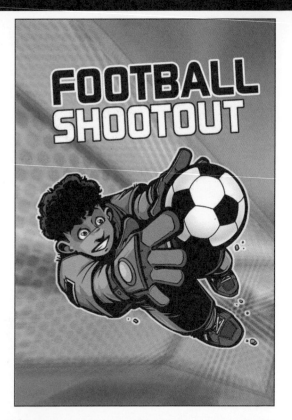

Ben always plays goalie for his football team. But when a new boy, James, moves to town, Ben has to play an unfamiliar position. James may have incredible talent, but he's also wildly unpredictable. Can the team survive the season?

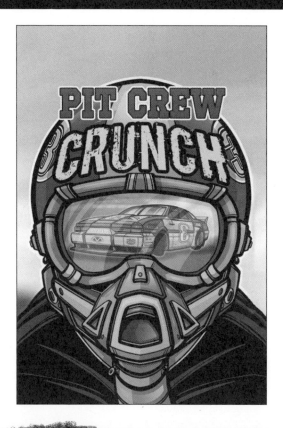

When Daniel wins a contest to be on a stock car pit crew, it's a dream come true! Soon he's spending his weekends at the racetrack, but when he finally gets his chance to work in a real race, things go wrong in a terrifying way...

FIND OUT MORE

Books

Extreme Snowboarding, Blaine Wiseman
(Weigl Educational Publishers Ltd, 2009)

Snowboarding, Andy Horsley
(ticktock Media, 2009)

To the Limit: Snowboarding, Paul Mason
(Wayland, 2008)

Website

www.snowboardclub.co.uk/learn
This website from Snowboard Club UK
has lots of information about learning to
snowboard.